THE DAY IT SNOWED

Jayne
Evans

Blackberry Lodge,
Coltshill Drive,
Newton
Mumbles
SA3 4SN

Jayne
Evans

I LOVE TO READ

The day it snowed

Translated and adapted by Irène D. Morris

Hans Peterson
Illustrated by Ilon Wikland

WORDS YOUR CHILDREN USE

First published in the English language September 1969
Reprinted 1984
© Burke Publishing Company Limited 1969
Translated and adapted from *När vi snöade inne*
© Hans Peterson 1960
Illustrations © Ilon Wikland 1960
Originally published in Swedish by Rabén & Sjögren, Stockholm

ISBN 0 222 79984 6 Hardbound
ISBN 0 222 79986 2 Paperback

Burke Publishing Company Limited
Pegasus House, 116–120 Golden Lane, London EC1Y 0TL, England.
Burke Publishing (Canada) Limited   *Registered Office:*
20 Queen Street West, Suite 3000, Box 30, Toronto, Canada M5H 1V5.
Burke Publishing Company Inc.   *Registered Office:*
333 State Street, PO Box 1740, Bridgeport, Connecticut 06601, U.S.A.
Printed in the Netherlands by Deltaprint Holland.

Contents

1

The Storm Begins

Tim lived in a big white house. All round the house were open fields, and beyond the fields was the forest. The main road was just by the edge of the forest.

From Tim's house it was twenty miles to the nearest town and five miles to the village. Tim had been to the town once with his parents. But that was a long time ago.

Tim had two sisters: Lorna who was twelve years old and Mary who was nearly nine. Tim himself was seven and a half.

He and his two sisters went to school in the village. Every morning, the school car collected them. Tim rather liked going to school by car. He liked the driver, Mr. Williams, too.

Mr. Williams always sang as he drove.

One morning, in early February, it started to snow. It snowed and snowed. Mary and Mother did not think that the school car would come.

"If it doesn't come," said Daddy, "I won't go to work either. I'll stay at home with you and have a day off."

Tim's father was a farmer. But he worked in the forest in the winter when there was no work to be done on the farm.

That morning, Tim, Mary and Lorna waited for a long time for the school car. Tim thought he would not mind if it never came. He did not really like school, though sometimes he thought

it was quite fun. But Mary loved school.
She wanted to go.

At last, the car arrived.

"I hope I can get you home again this
afternoon," said Mr. Williams, as he

dropped them off at the school. The children laughed. They did not believe that there could ever be so much snow that a car would not be able to drive through it.

But there was.

It snowed all day. Each breaktime, when they went outside, there was more snow. The snowflakes were bigger than any they had ever seen, and they kept coming, thick and fast. Tim and his friends Peter and Eric started to build a round snow-house, but they did not get it finished before the bell rang.

A wind had sprung up now. The snow was flying through the air. It had grown so dark indoors that they had to turn on the light.

When school was over for the day,
the children went to open the big front
door. But there was so much snow
pressing against it, that they found they

could not move it. Then Miss Brown tried. But she could not open it either. So all the children had to go out through Miss Brown's own private door at the back.

Miss Brown lived in the school-house. She had a little flat of her own. Her mother lived there too. Everybody called her mother "old Mrs. Brown". Old Mrs. Brown was sitting in the kitchen drinking tea when the children walked through. She smiled and nodded to them.

"Have you got your mittens on?" she asked.

"Yes, Mrs. Brown," they answered.

"Mr. Williams will drop the village children off before taking Tim, Lorna

and Mary home," said Miss Brown.
They said goodbye to her and
walked down the path to the road.
They had never seen so much snow
in their lives before. The ditches on
either side were completely covered
over, and it was impossible to tell

where the road ended and the fields began. Peter, who could never keep still, rushed off up the road. A moment later, he sank through the snow into a ditch. He sank right up to his arms. The other children started to laugh at him. He looked as if he were swimming in the deep snow. But then he started to cry. He could not get out by himself. Tim and Eric and Mary tried to help him. At last, they got him out. He was covered in snow from top to toe.

There was a sharp wind blowing. The children began to feel cold.

Miss Brown opened the window. "Hasn't the school car come yet?" she called out.

"No, we haven't seen it," the children called back.

"If it doesn't come soon, you will have to come back inside again," she cried.

The snowdrifts were like big waves. The snow whirled round the tops of the waves. Tim could not even see the houses across the road. They just looked like dark shadows. Behind the houses was an open field and the wind kept driving the snow across it. He felt almost afraid. He had never seen so much snow before. But it was exciting all the same.

The children stood between the high snowdrifts like a flock of lost sheep. They did not know what to do. But just as they were thinking of returning to the school-house, they heard the sound of an engine. It was the snow-plough, clearing the road. The children ran back towards the school. It was just as well they did, for the snow-plough was going very fast, throwing the snow high up in the air as it passed.

After the plough came the school car. All the children jumped in.

"I hope we can make it before the road disappears," said Mr. Williams. And this time, he did not sing. He drove very fast. The car skidded a bit on the snow-covered road, but he got them home safely.

Rollo, Tim's dog, was at the window,

barking his head off, when they arrived. Tim thought it was because he was angry with the snow. Or perhaps because he was afraid of it. It was so thick by now that the gate was completely hidden. Tim and Lorna and Mary climbed over the fence instead.

Daddy was not at home and Mother was a little worried. Soon after the children reached home, there was a terrible noise from the direction of the forest. When they looked out, they saw that an enormous pine-tree had blown down only a few yards from the garden. Mother grew more and more worried.

Mary and Lorna started to do their homework, but Tim went out for a while. He thought he might meet Daddy. He took the road past the stables. The four cows, Marigold, Daisy, Maggie and Bella, were all inside. The snow was so deep that Tim sank in up to his knees at each step he took.

When he had walked past the stables, he turned round again as he did not want to lose his way. But once he had turned, he did not know where he was. Everything looked so different.

And yet he had lived here, on the farm, all his life! He started to walk back in his own footsteps. But they very soon disappeared.

Tim stopped and looked around. The sheds were no longer there. The fence by the field had gone, too. He tried to look up, but the snow blew into his eyes. He could see nothing at all, and he did not even know if he was walking towards the house or away from it.

While Tim stood there, the snow grew thicker and thicker all around him. Just as he was beginning to feel really frightened, he heard Marigold mooing in the stables. The moment he heard her, Tim knew where he was, and he hurried off towards the house.

Rollo was asleep under the table when Tim came in. And Daddy was just taking off his boots. He had come in from the other side. Tim did not tell anybody about how he had nearly got lost just outside the house. He knew they would only tell him off.

2

Visitors

It snowed all night. Tim woke up early the next morning, and Mother told him that it had not stopped for a moment. When it was daylight, he saw the snow for himself.

"I'm staying at home today," said Daddy.

He had already been out and cleared the path from the kitchen door to the stables. But when Tim went out a few moments later the path was almost covered again.

"Rollo's kennel has disappeared," said Mary.

"And there's a snowdrift right across the kitchen window," said Lorna, pointing.

"Look at the blackberry bushes," said Mother. "You can't see them at all."

The fence by the road was covered, too. And it still kept on snowing.

"The snow-plough has been out all through the night," said Daddy. "But I don't think it will help much. It no sooner clears the road than the snow covers it up again."

"By the way, the telephone isn't working," said Mother.

"Perhaps a tree fell on the line and broke it," said Tim. He remembered that this had happened once.

"Perhaps," said Daddy. "Anyway, I don't think the school car will come today."

"Oh, good!" said Lorna, "I can help Mother make cakes."

"But I *want* to go to school," said Mary angrily.

Tim did not mind staying at home at all. He helped Daddy to clear the snow off the front steps and the path

down to the road. Just as they had finished, the snow-plough arrived. It pushed the snow off the main road into two high walls on either side. The walls of snow were taller than Daddy. And now they had to dig and shovel to try and get through it to the road.

It snowed all day. And the wind howled round the house.

"What terrible weather," said Mother and shook her head. "I feel sorry for all those poor people on the sea today."

"Yes, and on land, too, for that matter," said Daddy.

That morning was the last time Tim saw the snow-plough. After that, the snow became too deep for it to move. It was terribly cold and the wind was still blowing hard. The snow was very light and fluffy and, as soon as the plough had cleared it away, the wind blew it straight back again. In the afternoon, Tim and his father went out to look at the road. It was completely covered in snowdrifts, some of them seven feet tall.

In the middle of that night, there was a knock at the door. Tim woke up when Daddy went downstairs and put the light on. Rollo growled and barked.

Daddy opened the door. A man stood outside, covered in snow from head to foot. He was so white, he looked like a snowman.

"My car is stuck in the snow with my wife and two children in it," he said.

"I'll come and help you," said Daddy. He got dressed quickly. He pulled on his boots and lent the man from the car another pair. Tim, who had come down in his pyjamas, rushed back upstairs and dressed as quickly as he could. He wanted to come, too. Daddy just looked at him and said nothing. But he helped Tim on with his thick jacket and then they all three went outside. Tim held on to Daddy's hand. The air was full of white, whirling snowflakes. It was quite dark.

Tim's father did not bring a shovel. It would be no use, he said, trying to dig their way through. Instead, they all climbed over the high snowdrifts. A little way away, they could see the stranded car. It was a black car, but it was so covered with snow that it looked like a giant snowball. The windows were frosted over. They opened the door and a woman and two boys climbed out. The bigger of the two boys looked just a little younger than Tim. Daddy lifted up the smaller one and carried him, while the man put his arm round his wife and helped her along. The big boy walked on his own. Tim walked by his side, carrying the man's briefcase. It took them nearly half an hour to get back to the house.

By that time, Tim had made friends

with the bigger boy. His name was
Robert and he lived in the town. He
was not quite seven years old.

"But I am nearly as tall as you," he
said to Tim.

Robert was feeling very cold. He felt
cold all the way home.

"But I like snow, though," he said, "but I can't ski, but I have a pair of skis at home, but I don't use them."

Robert had a very funny way of

talking. He and Tim talked all the way back to the house.

When they arrived home, they found Tim's mother in the kitchen. She had made some hot chocolate and tea and sandwiches. Lorna and Mary moved in with Mother and gave their beds to the little boy and his mother. Robert shared Tim's bed and he fell asleep right away.

3

More Visitors

Soon it was morning again. Mother and Daddy had already been out and milked the cows by the time Tim got up. He played with Rollo in the kitchen for a while and then Robert woke up. Tim lent him a pair of old jeans and a pair of old brown boots that he had grown out of. And then, when they had had breakfast, the two boys set off in the snow towards the road. Very soon, they found another stranded car. Two men were sitting in it.

"You can come to our house if you like," said Tim.

"Thank you very much, but we don't dare to leave our car in case the snow-plough comes along and doesn't see it," said one of the men.

"You will get very cold," said Robert.

The men smiled but they stayed in the car. Tim and Robert walked on. The wind was howling and fresh snow kept falling. They saw several fallen trees, some of them lying across the road.

"If we had a saw," said Robert, "we could cut them in half, but we haven't, but it would be nice if we had."

"I'll tell Daddy to bring a saw along," said Tim.

34

Tim thought it was nice to have Robert as a friend. Robert talked and talked. He talked all the time they were walking.

Soon they came upon a red car. There were three people inside it, a man and two women. They wanted to come home with Tim. So Tim and Robert turned back and led them to the house.

Mary and Lorna were up and dressed. Mother gave the women some hot milk. Tim helped her put some extra mattresses on the floor for them. Then they fetched a pile of blankets and warmed them by the fire.

"This is terrible," said the man from the red car. "I have to be in town this afternoon."

Nobody answered him. Tim felt quite sorry for him, but Robert said, "Aren't you glad to be in here in this nice, warm house?"

The man did not answer and Tim wondered if he was angry. There was nothing to be done, though, for the snow just kept on falling. By now the snowdrifts were as high as the roof of the stables. Lorna and Mary helped Mother to lay the table, and to make tea and wash up.

Tim thought it was beginning to look like a hotel. There were strangers sitting about everywhere. Robert and Tim wanted to go out and look for more cars, but Mother told them to wait a little and have something to eat

first. Just then, three more lots of
people arrived. They said that they
had left their cars behind in the

snow. There were four men, two women and seven children. By the time they were all inside, the whole kitchen was filled with people. Rollo took one look at them and crawled under the table to hide.

The worst of it was that everybody was wet and cold. Tim and Lorna brought out all the thick woollen socks they could find. And warm, woollen cardigans and jumpers, too. The small children had to wear what was left over. But most of them were so hungry and tired that they just lay down on the mattresses on the floor and fell fast asleep. There were seven people in the bedroom. In the sitting-room, four people were lying round the fire and two small children were asleep in armchairs. The kitchen was filled with wet clothes hanging up to dry and Tim and Robert had to keep wiping the floor, because of the snow and water which dripped from the clothes.

Towards afternoon, Daddy took the saw and went out. Tim wanted to come, too. So did Lorna, but Mother said that she had to stay and help in the house because there was so much to do. Mother was making tea all day long and cooking potatoes in an enormous pot. Luckily, she had plenty of food because they had killed one of the pigs at Christmas.

"Can I come too?" asked Robert.

"I'd have to borrow Tim's boots again, but perhaps you don't want me to?"

"Of course you can," said Tim. He liked Robert. He was a bit small, but he was all right.

The three of them set off together. They soon reached the big tree which had fallen across the road. Tim's father stopped, and began to saw the tree in half. Tim and Robert walked on down the road for a while.

Near the big, open fields the road was completely blocked and rows of cars were stuck in deep snowdrifts. When Robert, Tim and his father returned home later on, they brought six men, eight women and eleven children with them. Mother looked quite frightened when she opened the door and saw them all. But she was soon hurrying off to bring out fresh cups and saucers and plates.

It was impossible for everybody to eat at the same time as there was not enough room. So all the children ate first. Robert talked the whole time he was eating. Some of the children did not want to eat, some of them screamed, one spilled food all over himself and another knocked a glass of milk over. In the end, there was such a noise that Tim could not hear a word Robert was saying, he could just see his mouth moving. Three boys started fighting and, just to add to the noise, Robert jumped up from the

table and began to bang two saucepan lids together.

Everybody was allowed to eat as many potatoes as they liked. But they could only have a very small piece of meat, because nobody knew how long they would have to stay. Then they each had some stewed apples. There was plenty of milk for everybody from the four cows.

It was a bit more difficult when it came to bed-time. There were twenty children, thirteen women and twelve men in Tim's house. That was more than all the children in the village school! Wherever Tim went, he fell over somebody sitting or lying or standing about. Some were talking and some were shouting and some of the children were crying. There was no danger of anybody getting lost in the forest tonight, Tim thought to himself, they would hear the noise for miles.

They put the mattresses in a row and then Daddy fetched some hay and spread it on the floor. In spite of the noise, all the children fell asleep and slept soundly.

44

4

Alone in the School-house

The snowstorm continued. Tim could not understand where all the snow came from. Robert thought that it must be the same snow going up and coming down again.

"This is no good," said one of the women after breakfast. "We must try and get away somehow."

"Yes," said one of the men, "I have to be in town this afternoon. It's very important."

"I would like to telephone home and tell them I'm safe," said another woman. "Is the telephone still not working?"

"No, and it may take weeks before they can mend it," said Mother.

"I'll ski down to the village," said Daddy, "and send telegrams if you like. We've all got skis in this family. We bought them for our skiing holidays."

Everybody gave Daddy long lists of names to send telegrams to. And Mother gave him a list of food to buy in the village shop. Daddy put a rucksack on his back and started off with Tim and Robert. Robert borrowed Mary's skis. Tim began to feel almost as if Robert were his brother. Robert wanted to join in everything. But he was not very good on skis. Tim could ski nearly as well

46

as his father, but Robert kept on
sliding this way and that. At first, he
spent most of the time flat on his face
in the snow. But after a while he grew
better at it. They travelled through
the forest, where the snow was thick
and firm.

The village looked just as if everybody were asleep. There were no bicycles to be seen, no cars and no people. Everyone was sitting at home by his fire. Daddy, Tim and Robert went to the post-office to send off all the telegrams. They were told it would take quite a while.

"Robert and I will go and see Miss Brown, then," said Tim.

So he and Robert set off. Robert was managing quite well on his skis by now—and if he had not talked so much he would have got on even better. Tim wondered if the village children had gone to school after all. But as soon as he reached the school-house, he saw that it was impossible to walk up the

48

path. Tim and Robert reached the front door on their skis. Then they found a spade and a shovel and started to clear away the snow. They worked very hard, and soon they had moved so much snow that they could open the door. They looked inside. It was dark and cold in the classroom. At first, they thought it was quite empty, but then they heard somebody move. They crept in very quietly, Tim first and then Robert. Robert held on to Tim's hand. Inside, in a rocking-chair, sat old Mrs. Brown. She had covered herself with blankets.

"Who's there?" she called out. "Is that you, Tim?"

"Yes," said Tim. "It's me, and

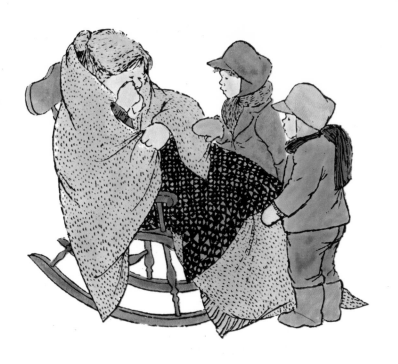

Robert from town. Where's Miss
Brown?"

Old Mrs. Brown did not answer at
once. And when she did, they could
hear that she was crying.

"I don't know, Tim," she said. "I
wish I did. She went out to take

Barbara home two days ago, because of the snowstorm, and she hasn't come back."

Barbara was in the same class as Lorna. She was twelve years old and she lived a long way away. Tim knew the way to her house. You had to get to it through the forest. It was not far from the place where he and Mary had built a den last summer.

"Perhaps Miss Brown stayed at Barbara's house. Perhaps there was too much snow for her to walk back."

"I tried to telephone," said old Mrs. Brown. "But their telephone is out of order."

"Our telephone doesn't work, either," said Tim.

Old Mrs. Brown sighed deeply.

"What terrible weather," she said. "I ran out of logs. I lit a log fire here in this classroom, but then I used all the logs up. There are plenty of logs in the shed, but I'm afraid of falling over if I go out."

"Don't you worry," Tim said. "Robert and I will fetch some logs. And then we'll call in on Barbara on our way home with Daddy. We'll tell Miss Brown that everything's all right here and that she had better stay the night. Otherwise she might get lost in the forest."

Tim and Robert hurried out of the classroom before old Mrs. Brown had time to answer. They put on their skis again, for the snow was far too deep to walk in. Then they struggled to open the door of the shed, which was piled high with snow. Robert tugged and pulled.

"My Mummy says, you can do *anything* if you really want to," he said.

"*Anything?*" said Tim. "I bet you can't. Have you ever tried to get the toothpaste back into the tube again?"

"No," said Robert, "but I'll try when I get home."

At last, they got the shed door open. They found a basket and started to fill it with logs. Robert was quite strong, though he was younger and smaller than Tim. He worked very hard. Together, they struggled across the snow

with the basket. They went back three times for more logs.

Old Mrs. Brown had already lit a fire and the classroom was beginning to be quite nice and warm.

Just at that moment, Daddy arrived.

Tim could see that he was worried when old Mrs. Brown told him that her daughter had not come back yet. But he did not say anything. He just left his rucksack on the front steps. Then they set off for Barbara's house.

Looking for Miss Brown

In the summer, Tim and Mary had often taken the path through the forest past Barbara's house. It had been an easy walk, then. But now they had to ski between the trees, with the wind and snow blowing in their faces. At last they got to Barbara's house. Barbara came to the door.

"Miss Brown isn't here," she said, and looked at them with frightened eyes. She told them that Miss Brown had stayed for a cup of tea and had then set off for home again.

Barbara's father, who was ill in bed,

wanted to get up and go out looking for her at once. But Tim's father would not let him. Instead, he and the two boys set off towards the village to find some men and organise a search-party.

"I don't think Miss Brown will have

gone very far," said Tim. "If she finds that she's lost, she'll just wait under some trees until the snow-storm is over."

"Perhaps she's sitting in the den that you and your sister built last summer," said Robert.

"Yes, maybe she's found it," said Tim. "She'd pass by it on her way back to the village."

"Let's go that way then," said Daddy. "That is, if you can find it, Tim."

Tim tried to find things that he recognized. At last, he found a big rock that he remembered. A little later, he thought he knew where he was and, at last, he felt sure that this was where the den ought to be.

They looked under the snow-covered branches, but they could find nothing. Daddy looked very worried. Tim did not know what to do next.

Robert went off among the trees calling, "*Miss Brown! Miss Brown!*" as loudly as he could.

"I don't think that will do much good," said Tim's father.

All the same, Tim started to shout, too.

"*Miss Brown! Miss Brown!*" he shouted at the top of his voice.

And, suddenly, there was an answering call from not very far away. It was Miss Brown! She had been sitting in

Tim's den all the time. It was just that Tim had been looking under the wrong tree.

Miss Brown had been in the den for almost two days, and she was terribly hungry and very tired. She had completely lost her way and had not dared to go any further. But she was quite all right.

She had lit a small fire and had covered the opening of the den with snow. So she had kept warm.

They all helped her to put on her skis and then Daddy almost carried her all the way back to the school. It was not very far really. In the summer, nobody could have got lost in that spot.

When they got back, old Mrs. Brown was so happy to see her daughter again that she began to cry. Tim and his father picked up the rucksack with the food and they all set off for home. They would not need a search-party after all.

Suddenly Robert stopped.

"Have you noticed something?" he asked.

They stopped and looked at him. And then they understood what he meant. It had stopped snowing. The wind had dropped, too. The air was cold and clear. It felt very strange. When they got home, it was almost dark. They had been away all afternoon.

The next morning, the snow-plough arrived again. It moved the snow off the road and threw it up into two, high walls. After that, the people who had been staying in Tim's house began to leave, one by one. Suddenly, the house was quite empty and quiet. Everybody had left. Everybody, that is, except Robert. His mother and father said that he could stay on for a week if he liked, and then they would come back and fetch him.

When everybody had left, Tim and Robert helped to tidy up. They carried the hay outside and cleaned the floor. And then Tim's mother went to bed. It was the first time Tim had ever seen his mother in bed in the daytime. She was so tired that she fell asleep at once and slept all that day and all night as well!

But the snow stayed. It stayed for a whole month. Soon, everybody grew so used to it that they did not even

notice it. The school car began coming again each morning.

During the week that Robert was there, he and Tim and Mary built a great fort in the snow. Tim was quite sure that it was the biggest snow-fort in the whole world. But then, they had had the biggest snowstorm in the whole world!